OUR pre-k pantry

Rosangela Perez

AuthorHouse™
1663 Liberty Drive
Bloomington, IN 47403
www.authorhouse.com
Phone: 833-262-8899

Because of the dynamic nature of the Internet, any web addresses or links contained in this book may have changed
since publication and may no longer be valid. The views expressed in this work are solely those of the author and do
not necessarily reflect the views of the publisher, and the publisher hereby disclaims any responsibility for them.

Any people depicted in stock imagery provided by Getty Images are models,
and such images are being used for illustrative purposes only.
Certain stock imagery © Getty Images.

This book is printed on acid-free paper.

ISBN: 979-8-8230-2897-4 (sc)
ISBN: 979-8-8230-2898-1 (hc)
ISBN: 979-8-8230-2899-8 (e)

Library of Congress Control Number: 2024912597

Print information available on the last page.

Published by AuthorHouse 11/18/2024

authorHOUSE®

Power
P.J
Julieta
Leena
Lani
Oscar
Dailen

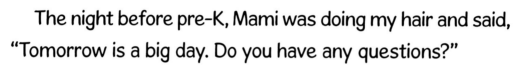

The night before pre-K, Mami was doing my hair and said, "Tomorrow is a big day. Do you have any questions?"

Without taking a breath, I asked, "Will the teacher be nice? Will my friends from Church Square Park be there? What if I have to go to the bathroom?"

Mami leaned my head back, kissed my forehead, and smiled. "Arriba, abajo, todo ese estrés para el lado."

After she tied off my hair, I turned and hugged her. I could smell her perfume, and it made me squeeze tighter. "I love you, Mami."

She always shared her calm with me.

After turning off the bathroom light, Mami walked with me to bed. She tucked me in and pulled out some books. I started to feel sleepy after a few stories and closed my eyes, so she finished the last one and tapped my nose gently.

"Dulces sueños, mi amor."

I opened my eyes to call her one more time.

"Mami, can we sing the song too? Seguro que sí dijo."

She stopped, moving back to my bed and placing a hand on my head as she began to sing.

Mi casita, mi casita, yo la quiero con amor, porque en ella, porque en ella es que aprendo lo mejor.

"Now, instead of *casita*, let's try *escuelita*," Mami suggested.

Mi escuelita, mi escuelita, yo la quiero con amor, porque en ella, porque en ella, es que aprendo la lección ...

4

When I woke up the next morning, Mami helped me get dressed and ready for the day. I ate breakfast with her while dancing to a cool song, giggling whenever she made a silly face or did a funny dance move. After a few songs, Mami stopped the music and let out a deep breath.

"All right. Chop, chop, lollipop. We have to get moving!"

I wanted to dance some more, and I wondered if I could dance at school too. "Mami wouldn't be at school, though, so who would I dance with? What if there was no dancing at all?

I wasn't sure I wanted to go to school anymore, standing in my spot and looking at my shoes. Mami leaned down and placed a hand on my head. She smiled. "Today will be a beautiful day in pre-K."

5

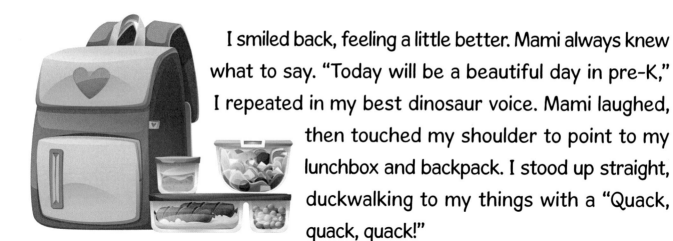

I smiled back, feeling a little better. Mami always knew what to say. "Today will be a beautiful day in pre-K," I repeated in my best dinosaur voice. Mami laughed, then touched my shoulder to point to my lunchbox and backpack. I stood up straight, duckwalking to my things with a "Quack, quack, quack!"

Mami got her keys while I held my backpack in one hand and my sweater in the other.

"I'll race you to the car," I said, running out the door. I heard her laughing behind me because I was super fast. My shoes made me even *faster*. Not as fast as the car when Mami started to drive, though. I looked out the window at all the stuff passing by, seeing people walking and talking just like Mami and me.

When we saw the crossing guard, Mami lowered the window so I could say "¡Hola!" when we drove by. I don't know if the guard heard me, but I think she did 'cause I waved a lot.

I was so excited, knowing it would be a good day. I got even more excited when I saw how cool my school was. Mami parked the car on Locust Street so we could walk across the street. She told me about my new teacher, Miss Z, and my classroom number. I was in room 107.

"Let's look for your teacher's name and number. Can you help me?"

I wanted to say yes, but there were a lot of people around, so I just got closer to Mami's legs, holding on to her.

The sound of a bell had me looking up and around. I saw a lady who looked like a nurse ringing it for everyone to hear. It made them stop talking and look at her. She had a sign in one hand, her voice loud and strong.

"Good morning! Let's line up, friends!"

Mami started walking with me toward the nurse. I did my best to be brave since Mami was brave too.

"We are going to have a beautiful day in pre-K!"

I gasped. "My mami says that!" I said, looking at the sign and tilting my head. "What does that say?"

The nurse smiled at me, pointing to each number and speaking slowly. "This says, 'Class one-oh-seven.' Is that your class?"

I nodded, amazed that she knew. "That's me! One-oh-seven."

The lady cheered and waved her hand so I would walk with her. "All right, follow me."

I looked up at Mami, and she nodded. I gave her a big bear hug, then I breathed in as if smelling a flower. I then breathed out as if blowing out a candle and waved goodbye to Mami as I followed the nurse into the school. We went up some stairs, and before I knew it, we were in a classroom where there was everything! First, there was a game. I had to find my picture in my cubby so I could put my stuff away.

After I finished, the nurse called everyone over to the rug. It had lots of squares and colors. When we all sat down, she tapped a box, and I heard it make a slow, soft sound.

"Good morning, boys and girls. I'm your new teacher, Miss Z. This is Miss A, and she is also going to be your teacher this year. We are so happy to be here with you in pre-K today! Does anyone have any questions so far?"

I looked around, raising my hand high so she could see. "Are you a nurse or a teacher?"

She chuckled. "Good observation, Tony. I do look like a nurse. That's because I am wearing clothes called scrubs. Nurses wear them to work. I like to wear them, too, because they're comfortable. I can learn new things and remember better that way. What about everyone else? How do you learn best?"

Some of my friends were really excited, talking a lot to the new teachers. Some of them weren't as excited, though, not talking at all and looking at the carpet or around the room. I think they were shy like me when I first saw the school.

Miss Z tapped the wooden box again. "OK, boys and girls. Let's explore the classroom. Meet back here when you hear the sound of this red timer. It will make a sound like '*Beep! Beep! Beep!*' Can you repeat that sound?"

Everyone started to beep.

"OK, off you go. Have fun exploring your classroom!"

*****

Back on the rug, Miss Z asked, "What did you see? What do you think will be one of your favorite spaces to work in?"

Lydia raised her hand and said, "I like the store."

Food Pyramid for Kids

4 Fats and
   Sugar

3 Dairy
   Group

2 Fruits and
   Vegetables

1 Grain
   Group

Atlas, Victoria, Price, Julieta, Carlitos, Mateo, Javen, Lidia,Leena, Allie, Avianna, Abraham, Power, Abril

Miss Z asked Lydia to show her where the store was and waved her arm to us. We all followed.

"Good job, Lydia! This does look like a store, but this is what we call our pre-K pantry. Repeat after me, my friends: 'pre-K pantry.' This pantry is special because here, we keep free and healthy snacks for you all. We also have water, small juices, forks, napkins, and cups in case we forget our snack or if we didn't have breakfast. We can even use it when we need a little something to give us energy."

I nodded as I looked around at all the stuff in the pantry.

"We have to share what is in our pantry and help keep it neat," Miss Z explained. It felt important to remember.

"Do you want to know a secret?" asked Miss A. "The pantry will also help you learn to read. And the best part is that you get to taste new snacks. Will you help Miss Z and me do that?

"Yes!" everyone cheered.

The rest of our morning in pre-K was very busy. We were able to go and work in several learning areas. We read stories in the book area, explored in the discovery area, worked in the house area, and built in the block area. The teachers said we would continue to explore the classroom tomorrow, which made me excited to come back and see what else I could find.

Before I knew it, it was snack time, and I was super hungry. There was a picture on the board with a song that said, "Time to eat."

"OK, friends. Get your snack bags, find a chair, and chat with your friends about your first day in pre-K!"

Miss A repeated her words in Spanish, and I walked to my backpack to find my lunchbox. I stopped and felt my face get hot when I couldn't find it, looking one more time. I turned around and saw my friends sitting and eating. I began to cry near my cubby.

Miss Z walked over, leaning down. "Tony? You look sad. Can I help?"

I sniffed and pointed at my backpack, feeling sad all over again. "I ... don't ... have ... my ... snack bag!"

Miss Z made a surprised face. "Oh, sweetie."

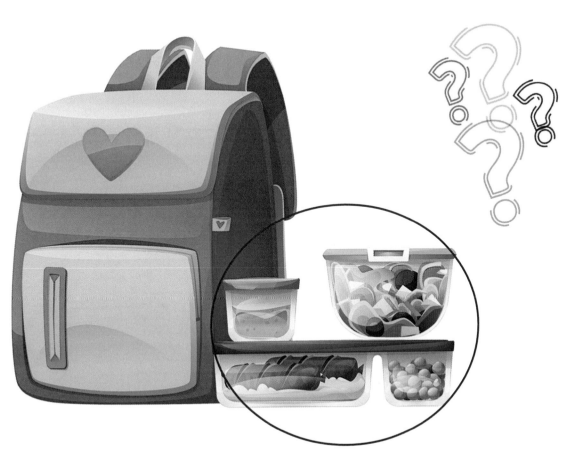

She gave me a hug, which made me feel a little better. "We can go get something from our pre-K pantry, OK? Don't worry, my love."

She gave me another hug and patted my back. She stood up, leading the way to the pantry. I chose cookies that looked like flowers and a water bottle. It reminded me to smell my flowers and blow out my candles.

"Thank you, Miss Z. I love our pre-K pantry."

Miss A rang a blue bell.

"Time to go home! Line up, friends."

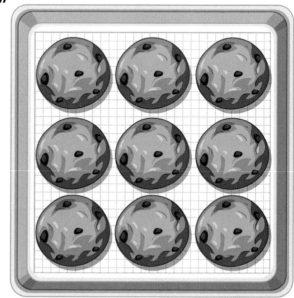

After lining up and walking outside, I ran to Mami and gave her a big bear hug and a kiss. On the drive home, I told her all about the classroom, my friends, and Miss A and Miss Z. When we got back home, I ran over to where my lunchbox was, holding it up. "Mami, I forgot my snack today! Look, it's still here!"

Her eyes looked bigger as she put her keys down. "Are you hungry? What did you eat today?"

I told her all about the pre-K pantry and the flower cookies and water I got.

"I was the first to use it, and we have to keep it neat so when friends forget a snack, they have one too. It has all the things we have. It looks like a store!"

The more I talked about it, the more excited I was to go back to school. I liked pre-K. I liked it so much that after my nighttime books and a song, I dreamed about my friends, my teachers, and our pre-K pantry.

Printed in the United States
by Baker & Taylor Publisher Services